This sakhi book belongs to:

....

This book was devised, designed and completed by volunteers from
Sikh History And Religious Education (S.H.A.R.E.)

Illustrations by Cristian Rodriguez.

All rights reserved. This book may not be reproduced in whole or in any part in any
form without permission from S.H.A.R.E. ©

Published by Sikh History and Religious Education

Registered Charity Number: 1120428

Khalsa@sharecharityuk.com

Bibi Harsharan Kaur

Dedicated to every woman who has lived and died for a righteous cause; Your actions continue to inspire us all

This is a <u>sakhi</u> from the time of <u>Guru Gobind Singh Jee</u>. Sikhs wanted everyone to have the right to practise their religion freely and live however they wished.

Bibi Harsharan Kaur became a <u>Kaur</u> when she was very young. She loved Guru Jee very much and wanted to make Guru Jee happy so she did her <u>paath</u> and <u>simran</u> every day. She never told lies and respected everyone equally.

Bibi Harsharan Kaur was very strong and brave. She ate her vegetables and fruit every day.

In the year 1704, Guru Gobind Singh Jee and His forty Singh's battled the <u>Mughal army</u> at <u>Chamkaurs mud fort</u>. During the battle, many of the Mughal soldiers were hurt. Thirty-six of Guru Jee's soldiers were <u>Shaheed</u>. This included his two eldest sons, <u>Baba Ajit Singh</u> and <u>Baba Jujhar Singh.</u>

Guru Jee was requested to leave the fort by the <u>Panth Khalsa</u> (in the form of the <u>Panj Pyaare)</u>. After leaving the battlefield, Guru Jee travelled eventually arriving at Talvandee Sabo (Damdama Sahib).

The Mughals thought Guru Jee had left this earth, and started spreading rumours in the villages.

"Gobind Singh is no more! Gobind Singh is no more! His family is also finished. No one is allowed to <u>cremate</u> the remaining Singhs at Chamkaur. We have sealed the area!".

The Mughals were going from village to village telling everyone that the <u>revolution</u> had died with Guru Gobind Singh Jee.

Many people were scared and went back to their homes.

However, not so far away in the village Khroond, Bibi Harsharan Kaur was saddened to hear that the remaining Shaheed Singhs were lying in the fields of Chamkaur.

She asked her mother, "Mummy Jee, please can I have permission to go and cremate the Shaheed Singhs? I cannot leave my brothers there."

Her mother replied, "It's very dark and cold outside. There are Mughal soldiers everywhere. How will you ever get near?"

Guru Gobind Singh Jee's daughter, Bibi Harsharan Kaur replied, "MummyJee, I must go, even if I get hurt trying – I will try my very best to avoid the soldiers".

Hearing her brave daughter, her mother thought, "She is a daughter of the <u>Khalsa</u>. She is brave and strong".

Her mother kissed her forehead, and explained the <u>Maryada</u> for performing the Sikh cremation ceremony.

When she arrived she looked for men with <u>Karay</u> on their wrists, <u>Kachaaray</u> and long <u>Kesh</u>. This was the only way to know the difference between the Sikh soldiers and everyone else.

Every time she found a Shaheed Singh, she would say <u>Vaheguru Jee Ka Khalsa Vaheguru Jee Kee Fateh</u> and wipe his face. She would then carefully and quietly take each body to an area where the cremations were carried out.

She repeated this for every Shaheed Singh, including the eldest Sahibzadey, Baba Ajit Singh and Baba Jujhar Singh. She then collected wood and lit the fire.

The Mughal soldiers saw the flames from far away. They ran towards the flames and to their surprise saw a woman standing alone by the <u>pyre</u>.

Bibi Harsharan Kaur was reciting <u>Kirtan Sohela</u>. The Mughals asked her, "Who are you?" .

She finished her paath and replied, "I am the daughter of Guru Gobind Singh Jee". "What are you doing here?" the soldier asked. "I am cremating my Shaheed brothers" she replied.

"It is a crime to come here!" shouted the soldier. Bibi Harsharan Kaur replied "I only follow orders of the True King—Guru Gobind Singh Jee".

The soldiers were angry when they heard Bibi Jee's words. Suddenly, the soldiers tried to capture her. Bibi Harsharan Kaur grabbed her <u>Kirpan</u> and defended herself. She was fighting them off strongly. The Mughal soldiers picked her up and threw her on to the pyre with her Singh brothers.

The next day the blockade around Chamkaur was lifted. News of Bibi Harsharan Kaur's <u>seva</u> reached Guru Gobind Singh Jee at Talvandee Sabo (Damdama Sahib).

Bibi Harsharan Kaur was 19 years old. She loved her Guru and His soldiers so much, she <u>sacrificed</u> her life to ensure they were not left on the field of Chamkaur.

Bibi Harsharan Kaur got her bravery from all the paath and simran she did. If you want to be brave like her, remember to do your Mool Mantar and at least five minutes Vaheguru Simran every day.

Bibi Harsharan Kaur also got her strength from eating lots of vegetables, fruits and daal. If you want that super-duper strength, don't forget to eat lots of superfoods!

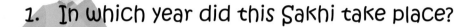

Lets See what you learnt!

1. In which year did this Sakhi take place?

   _____

2. What was the name of the battlefield in this sakhi?

   _____

3. What are the names of Guru Jee's two eldest sons?

   _____

4. How did Bibi Harsharan Kaur recognise the Sikh soldiers?

   _____

5. How did Bibi Harsharan Kaur become so brave and strong?

   _____

WELL DONE!

Glossary

Amrit : Ambrosial Nectar (immortal)

Ardas : Supplication, prayer to God

Baba Ajit Singh : Elder son of 10th Guru

Baba Jujar Singh : Elder son of 10th Guru

Chamkaur mud fort : Ropar district of the Punjab was the scene of two battles

Cremate: The way Sikhs conduct last rites

Guru Gobind singh Jee: 10th Guru of the Sikhs and creator of the Khalsa

Kachaara(y): Cotton undershorts/undergarment which resemble boxer shorts are one of the five Sikh articles of faith

Kara(y): Iron bangle, one of the five Sikh articles of faith

Kaur: Princess or Lioness. Name given to female when given Amrit

Kesh : Uncut hair

Kirpan: Kirp—Mercy Aan—Honour. Worn by baptised Sikhs

Kirtan Sohela: night time prayer said by all Sikhs before they go to sleep

Khalsa: Pure, someone who has received Amrit

Maryada: conventional religious rules and rites

Mool Mantar: Mool—root Mantar - magic chant
Mughal (Army): Islamic empire, ruled over India since 1526
Paath: Sikhi Prayer(s)
Panj Pyaare: Five Beloved ones
Panth Khalsa: worldwide community of Khalsa or Sikhs generally
Pyre: structure, usually made of wood, for burning a body
Revolution: change in power or organisational structure
Sacrifice: Bloodless or blood offering (in the Name of God)
Sakhi: Real life historical event relating to Sikhi
Shaheed: Person who suffers and endures death on behalf of a belief or faith
Seva: Selfless service
Simran: Meditation on Gods Name
Singh: Lion. Name given to male when given Amrit
Vaheguru: Vah—wonderful Guru—God
Vaheguru Jee Ka Khalsa Vaheguru Jee Kee Fateh: The Pure ones belong to God victory belongs to God.